Karen's Big Weekend

Look for these
and other books about Karen
in the
Baby-sitters Little Sister series

Little Sister

Karen's Big Weekend
Ann M. Martin

Illustrations by Susan Tang

A
LITTLE **APPLE**
PAPERBACK

SCHOLASTIC INC.
New York Toronto London Auckland Sydney

ISBN 0-590-47043-4

12 11 10 9 8 7 6 5 4 3 2 1   3 4 5 6 7 8/9

Printed in the U.S.A.   40

First Scholastic printing, December 1993

This book is in honor of the birth of
James Lovell Hemphill
Welcome!

The Surprise

"The turkey ran away," sang my little brother, "before Thanksgiving Day. Said he they'll make a roast of me if I should stay."

"Andrew, you can quit singing Thanksgiving songs now," I told him. "Thanksgiving is over. Christmas is coming."

"I know," said my brother. "I just like that song." He went back to his coloring. But he began to hum "Jingle Bells" instead.

I think Christmas is my favorite holiday. I like all holidays, but I like Christmas best. It comes at the same time of year as a lot of other holidays — Thanksgiving and Hanukkah and New Year's Eve. Also, it comes at the start of winter, and that means snow. Snowmen and snowflakes and snowballs, and snow walks after dark.

I was looking forward to Christmas, and I was hoping for lots of snow. "Frosty the Snowman," I sang.

"Rudolph, the Red-Nosed Reindeer," sang Andrew.

That night, Andrew and I sat down to supper with Mommy and Seth. Seth is our stepfather. We like him.

I looked out the window. "Hey, it's snowing!" I cried.

"Indoor voice, Karen," said Mommy.

"Sorry," I said. Then I whispered, "Hey, it's snowing."

Andrew was peering out the window. "It *is* snowing," he said.

I am Karen Brewer. I am seven years old. I am in second grade. I have blonde hair and blue eyes and some freckles. I wear glasses. I even have two pairs. The blue pair is for reading. The pink pair is for the rest of the time. (Well, I do not have to wear them when I am asleep.)

Andrew is four going on five. He is only in preschool, but he can already read. Guess who taught him to read. Me! I must be a very good teacher. That is probably because I have a very good teacher myself. Her name is Ms. Colman. She is the best teacher ever.

Seth was serving our dinner. Mommy was standing by her place at the kitchen table. "Karen, Andrew," she said. "Seth and I have a surprise for you."

Andrew and I stopped looking at the snow. "You do?" I said.

"Yes," replied Mommy. She sat down. "In one week we will have a special Christmas treat. We are going to go to New York City for the weekend. We will look at the big Christmas tree and see the other decorations. And we will go to the theatre to see a play."

"Will we eat in restaurants?" asked Andrew.

"Of course," said Seth.

"Can we visit Maxie?" I asked.

Maxie is Maxie Medvin. She is my pen pal, and she lives in New York City. Maxie and I have been writing to each other ever since the kids in Ms. Colman's class began a pen pal project with the kids in a New York City class. We even met each other once, when Maxie's class took a field trip here to Stoneybrook, Connecticut. But Maxie and I have not seen each other since then.

"Can we visit Maxie?" Mommy repeated. She glanced at Seth. "Hmm. We had not thought about that. We will see."

Mommy and Seth told us some more about our trip. They talked about museums and Central Park and glittery Christmas decorations and a Santa Claus on every street corner.

I decided this was going to be the best Christmas ever.

Maxie Medvin

Guess what. When Maxie Medvin and I first became pen pals, we did not like each other very much. Maxie told me she was already eight years old. (I am only seven.) She said she has big sisters who are twins. (I only have one big sister.) She has two adopted little brothers. (I only have one adopted little sister.) She has been to Disney World *and* Disneyland. (I have only been to Disney World.) So I decided I needed to make myself sound more interesting. I wrote some things to Maxie that

5

were not quite true. In fact, they were lies. Then Maxie made up some lies, so I made up more lies, and pretty soon we were in a big mess. But after we met each other we became friends. Now we *still* write to each other, and we would like to see each other again soon. (We do not lie anymore.)

That night, I asked Mommy about Maxie again. "*Please*, can we visit her?" I begged. "I cannot go to New York and not see Maxie. That would be silly. Besides, I *really* want to see where she lives, and meet her sisters and brothers."

"We-ell," Mommy said.

"Can I at least call her?" I went on. "I want to tell her about our trip."

Mommy let me call Maxie.

"Hi, Maxie!" I cried, when she was on the phone. "Guess what. In one week I am coming to New York! I am coming for the weekend with my family."

"That's great!" said Maxie. "Which family?"

"Mommy's," I replied. (Maxie knows I have two families. I will tell you about them later.)

"What are you going to do on your trip?" asked Maxie.

"Oh, everything. See the Christmas decorations, go to a play."

"Can you come visit me?" asked Maxie.

"I hope so," I replied.

Pretty soon Mommy asked to get on the telephone. She wanted to speak to Mrs. Medvin. Then Seth talked to Mr. Medvin. When he was finished, he gave the phone back to me. "Here is Maxie," he said. "She has a surprise for you."

"Guess what!" exclaimed Maxie. "When you are in New York, you are going to come over to my apartment on Friday night!"

"We are?"

"Yes. The grown-ups talked about it. You and your family are going to meet me and my family. Then we are going to go out to dinner, and then maybe we will go to the

Christmas show at Radio City Music Hall. That means we will spend the whole evening together."

"Cool!" I cried. "What restaurant are we going to eat at? Can we go to Mamma Leones? I have seen that on TV."

"I don't know," replied Maxie. "I will have to ask Mom and Dad about that. But anyway, you know what else your parents said? They said on Saturday, the next day, you can come over to my apartment by yourself. They will drop you off and we can play together."

A play date with Maxie in New York City. This was very cool. "What will we do?" I asked.

"Oh, we can play in my room. Or maybe someone will take us to Central Park, or even out for ice cream."

"Great! Maxie, I cannot wait to see you!"

"I cannot wait to see you either."

"Well, I better go," I said. "I want to call the big house."

I had news for my other family.

Cool, I cried. What I meant are we

A Two-Two Christmas

Most people have just one family, but I have two. I am part of Mommy's family at the little house, and I am part of Daddy's family at the big house. I did not always have two families, though. A long time ago, when I was a very little kid, I had one family: Mommy, Daddy, Andrew, and me. We lived at the big house. (That is the house Daddy grew up in.) Then Mommy and Daddy started fighting. They fought and fought and fought. Finally they decided to get a divorce. They said they loved Andrew and me very much, but they did not love each other anymore. And they could not live together anymore. So Mommy moved into a little house, and Daddy stayed in his big house. Now Andrew and I live at the little house most of the time. We live at the big house every other weekend and on some holidays and vacations.

We have a family at each house. This is because Mommy and Daddy have gotten married again, but not to each other. Mommy married Seth. That is how he became our stepfather. Daddy married Elizabeth. She is our stepmother.

This is who is in my little-house family: Mommy, Seth, Andrew, me, Rocky, Midgie, and Emily Junior. Rocky and Midgie are Seth's cat and dog. Emily Junior is my pet rat.

This is who is in my big-house family: Daddy, Elizabeth, Andrew, me, Kristy, Charlie, Sam, David Michael, Emily Michelle, Nannie, Shannon, Boo-Boo, Goldfishie, and Crystal Light the Second. Kristy,

10

Charlie, Sam, and David Michael are Elizabeth's kids, so they are my stepsister and stepbrothers. They are all older than me. (Well, David Michael is only a few months older.) Emily Michelle is my adopted sister. She is two and a half. She was born far away in the country of Vietnam. (I named my rat after her.) Nannie is Elizabeth's mother, so she is my stepgrandmother. The others are pets. Shannon is a big floppy puppy, and Boo-Boo is an old tomcat. Can you guess what Goldfishie and Crystal Light are? (Andrew named Goldfishie.)

I have special nicknames for my brother and me. I call us Andrew Two-Two and Karen Two-Two. (I thought of those names after my teacher read a book to our class. It was called *Jacob Two-Two Meets the Hooded Fang*.) We are two-twos because we have two houses and two families, two mommies and two daddies, two cats and two dogs. We also have two of lots of other things. I have two bicycles, one at each house. (An-

11

drew has two trikes.) We have clothes and books and toys at each house. Plus, I have those two pairs of glasses. I even have two best friends. They are Nancy Dawes and Hannie Papadakis. Nancy lives next door to Mommy. Hannie lives across the street from Daddy and one house down. We are all in Ms. Colman's second-grade class at Stoneybrook Academy. (We call ourselves the Three Musketeers.)

Most of the time I like being a two-two. I love both of my families. But sometimes being a two-two is hard. When I am at Mommy's, I miss my big-house family. When I am at Daddy's, I miss my little-house family. Then there is the holiday problem. Everyone wants Andrew and me to celebrate the holidays with them. Usually we have two Thanksgivings and two Christmases and two birthdays and even two Halloweens. One at each house. This might sound like fun, but sometimes Andrew and I get very, very tired. Even so, I was looking forward to our two-two Christmas this year. It is hard not to feel excited about Christmas. And now I could also look forward to Christmas in New York. In one week I would visit Maxie Medvin in the big city!

Christmastime in New York City

"Mommy," said Andrew one day, "tell me again what we are going to do in New York City."

This was about the tenth time Andrew had said that. So Mommy replied, "Andrew, I have an idea. I know a book we should read before we go to New York. Karen, you will like it, too. Let's see if we can find it at the library."

Mommy drove Andrew and me to the public library. Sure enough, we found a book called *Christmastime in New York City*.

It was by a woman named Roxie Munroe. We sat down at a table and looked at the book.

"See?" said Mommy. "There is the big tree. And there are the store windows with their decorations. Look at the crowds in the city."

"Lots and lots of people," said Andrew.

Mommy checked the book out and we brought it home with us.

Almost every night after dinner my little-house family talked about the things we would do in New York. We looked at Roxie Munroe's book a lot. Seth showed us an old picture book that *he* had read when *he* was little. It was called *This Is New York*. Andrew and I liked the drawings of the tall, tall buildings. "They are called skyscrapers," Seth told us.

"Skryscrapers," said Andrew. (He just could not say the word right.)

Our trip to New York was going to begin on a Friday morning. We would get on a train right after breakfast. Andrew and I were not even going to go to school that day.

On Thursday afternoon Hannie and Nancy came to my house to help me pack. Also, the Three Musketeers had to say good-bye to each other.

"We will miss you in school tomorrow," said Nancy.

"Thank you," I replied politely. "I will be thinking about you on the train. And I will think about you in New York City."

"How much do you have to pack to go to New York?" asked Hannie. She was looking at my bulging suitcase.

"Oh, plenty," I replied.

Hannie opened the suitcase. She peered inside. Then she began counting. Finally she said, "*Seven* dresses? You will only be gone for three days, Karen."

"I spill a lot," I told her. But I did unpack a few dresses. And then I decided I only needed two pairs of shoes (not five), one

16

book (not eight), and one stuffed animal (not six).

When I finished packing, I set the suitcase on the floor. Hannie and Nancy and I sat on my bed.

"I cannot believe Christmas is almost here," said Hannie.

"And tonight is the first night of Hanukkah," added Nancy.

"Is it true you get presents for *eight* nights?" asked Hannie.

"Yup," replied Nancy. "But that is not what Hanukkah is really about."

"You know what I decided to do?" I spoke up. "I decided to buy your presents in New York. I will have very wonderful gifts to give you at our party."

Nancy and Hannie and I were going to have a holiday party, just for us, the Three Musketeers. We were going to hold it on a Saturday in between Hanukkah and Christmas.

"Presents from New York?" said Nancy. "Cool!"

I thought so. Plus, I had saved and saved my money, and now I had almost fifteen dollars to spend just on Hannie and Nancy. That was a fortune. There was no telling what I could buy.

The Big Apple

"Oof! Karen, your suitcase weighs a ton," said Seth. "What did you pack?"

"Not that much," I replied. "I even took *out* a lot of stuff yesterday." (I had put some of it back in, though. I guess the suitcase *was* a little heavy.)

It was Friday morning. My family and I were ready to leave for New York. Seth was putting our suitcases in the car. And it was still dark outside. Mommy had meant it when she said we would leave early.

"Good-bye! Good-bye!" I called to Rocky

and Midgie and Emily Junior as Mommy backed down the driveway. "Behave yourselves for Nancy!" Nancy and her parents were going to take care of our pets until we came home on Sunday.

We drove to the station. We stood on the platform and shivered while we waited for our train to arrive. Andrew and I watched our breath puff out in front of us. Andrew pretended he was a fire-breathing dragon.

A lot of other people were waiting for trains, too. Mostly they were grown-ups carrying briefcases. Mommy said they were probably going to their offices in Stamford or New York City.

Toot! Toot!

"Here comes the train!" shrieked Andrew. "I hear its whistle!"

"And I see its headlight!" I cried.

"Settle down, kids," said Mommy.

We struggled onto the train with our suitcases and bags.

"Here we go," said Seth. "Four seats together." He and Mommy piled our things onto the luggage racks.

"May I give our tickets to the conductor?" asked Andrew. Andrew just loves conductors. He has decided he wants to be one when he grows up.

"Sure," replied Mommy. But she waited until the conductor was standing next to us before she gave Andrew the tickets.

The conductor was a woman. She called Andrew sir.

"Thank you, sir," she said to him.

"We are going to New York City," I told her.

"Ah. The Big Apple," she replied. "Did you know that's the city's nickname? And New York is called the Empire State."

"Like in *The Empire Strikes Back*?" I said. "Cool."

The ride to New York seemed long. Andrew and I fell asleep. But we woke up before we pulled into the station. We were flying along underground. I could see only

darkness outside the windows.

Screech. The train finally came to a stop. The doors opened. We walked into the biggest, most crowded station I had ever seen. Guess what. Stores were everywhere.

"Stores in a train station?" I said.

"Restaurants, too," replied Seth.

"Oh, boy," I said.

I held tightly to Seth's hand. Andrew held tightly to Mommy's. We did not want to be separated from the grown-ups. Not in that big crowd.

Seth was hurrying us out of the station, but I kept slowing down to look in the store windows. "Hey!" I cried as I paused in front of one. "Can we go in there? *Please?* I see something for Hannie and Nancy."

The four of us went into the store and I bought two tiny buttons. Each one said I ♥ NYC. Hannie and Nancy would love them. And I still had $14.11 to spend on their real presents.

We left the station then, and Mommy

hailed a cab. We piled into it. "Stanmark Hotel, please," said Mommy, and we were off. I stared at the people and the buildings and the traffic. New York was a very busy place.

Oh, Christmas Tree

The trip to the hotel went by in a flash. I was so busy looking out the window that I did not say one word until the taxi pulled to a stop. "Here you go, Stanmark Hotel," said the driver.

Our room in the hotel was very beautiful. Andrew and I wanted to stay in it for awhile. We wanted to fill the ice bucket and unwrap the little bars of soap. Also, we had a million questions. For instance, what was a coffee maker doing in the bathroom?

But Mommy said, "Come on, kids. Let's

go. We do not want to waste time in the hotel. Put on your walking shoes."

And Seth said, "We have big plans today. There is a lot to see and do."

So we put on our sneakers and bundled up in our coats and left the hotel. Our first stop was going to be a place called Rockefeller Plaza.

"That is where the Christmas tree is," said Mommy.

We walked along a bustling street. I tried to read the street signs. We were on Fifth Avenue. I knew that was famous.

Mommy and Seth kept pointing things out. "There's Brentano's Bookstore. There's St. Patrick's Cathedral. There's Saks Fifth Avenue."

Andrew and I were trying to peer in the windows of Saks, which is a very big department store, when Seth said, "Okay, kids. Turn around and look across the street."

Andrew and I turned. I gasped. There it was. The Christmas tree. It was covered with lights, thousands of them. A star shone on the top. I was sure it was the biggest Christmas tree in the world.

"Let's cross the street so we can see better," suggested Mommy.

When we had crossed the street we stood on the edge of the sidewalk. I looked between a double row of angels playing trumpets. I could see the tree at the other end. But something was between the angels and the tree. We walked closer. The ice-skating rink! The tree stood over a skating rink. Now I remembered it from Roxie Munroe's pictures. Far below us the skaters glided and turned and slipped and slid. Above them the tree shone. I was sure I was in the most wonderful and Christmasy place ever.

After we had watched the skaters for awhile Mommy said, "Is anybody hungry? Let's get a special treat."

I clutched Mommy's hand as we walked back toward the street. Mommy stopped by a man with a pushcart. "Four pretzels,

please," she said. "Two plain, two with mustard."

The man handed us the pretzels and Mommy paid him. My pretzel was gigundo! They all were. And it was salty and warm and . . . soft. I had never eaten a *soft* pretzel. Only hard, crunchy ones.

We returned to Fifth Avenue and walked along the street again.

We saw Christmas trees and candles and menorahs in almost every window. Then, suddenly, I looked up. Hanging above my head was an enormous glittery snowflake. Just hanging in the air over an intersection. (Everything about New York seemed *big*.)

"There it is," said Seth. "There is New York's snowflake."

Behind it, at the entrance to a park, was another *big* decoration. It was a giant menorah, much taller even than Seth. I looked at the menorah. I looked back at the snowflake. I thought of the Christmas tree. "I just love New York," I announced.

Mommy smiled at me. "I'm glad you are having fun," she said.

"Okay, let's go shopping," I replied.

We looked in some of the stores near the snowflake, but I did not see any presents that looked *just* right for Nancy and Hannie. Oh, well. We were going to be in New York for two more days. We would have plenty of time to shop.

Where Is Andrew?

After we had finished our pretzels, and looked at the snowflake and the menorah and some stores, it was Andrew's naptime. He was cranky. But no one wanted to go back to the hotel, including Andrew.

"Maybe you just need a little rest," Mommy said to him. "Why don't we go to Lord and Taylor to look at their Christmas windows. But instead of walking there we will take the bus. That way you can sit down for a little while."

I thought this was a great idea. I wanted

31

to see what the inside of a New York City bus looked like. And in just a few minutes we were on one, riding back down Fifth Avenue the way we had come. I liked the bus a lot. The seats faced the aisle, not the driver. You could kneel backward in your seat and look out the window. And the bus had two doors, one in front and one in back. Plus, when someone wanted to get off, he pulled on a rope, a bell rang, and the driver stopped the bus.

As we rolled down Fifth Avenue, Mommy and Seth pointed out some of the things we had already seen. "There is the tree again! There is St. Patrick's! There is Brentano's Bookstore!" Then Mommy pointed out something new. "There is the Public Library," she said. "See the lions?"

"Lions? What lions?" Andrew sat up fast. He had been lying down with his head in Seth's lap. But now he peered out the window.

So did I. My brother and I saw two great

stone lions perched in front of a wide building with lots of steps.

"I thought you meant real lions," said Andrew. But he did not sound disappointed. He looked and looked at those lions. They were wearing Christmas wreaths around their necks.

"I think they are guarding the library," I said to Mommy.

"Oh, there is Lord and Taylor!" exclaimed Mommy. "Come on. Everybody off the bus!"

We scrambled toward the back door and hopped down the steps. We found ourselves in front of a department store.

"Another *store*?" whined Andrew.

"Yes, but we are not going inside it. What we want to see is right out here. In the windows. Let's get on line," said Mommy.

In Stoneybrook the store windows look very pretty at Christmastime. But people do not line up to see them. The people in front of Lord and Taylor stood in a line that wound around like the ones at Disney World. We waited and waited. As soon as I saw the first window I understood why everyone else wanted to see the windows, too.

"Ooh," I gasped.

I was holding Mommy's hand. We were looking at the inside of a fancy house at Christmastime. I forgot it was just a window decoration. People moved. A puppy jumped up and down. The lights on a tree blinked on and off. The next window looked like a winter wonderland with children skating on a pond and building a snowman and throwing snowballs. Another window showed an old-fashioned general store.

I could have gazed in the windows for hours, but the line kept moving, and soon we had walked past the store. I looked around me. Then I looked up at Mommy and Seth.

"What did you think?" asked Seth.

"That was great," I said. "But where is Andrew?"

We did not see him.

Andrew was missing.

Santa Claus

Mommy and Seth and I looked up and down the sidewalk. Seth dashed around a corner. "I do not see him!" he cried when he ran back.

"Andrew! Andrew!" Mommy and Seth and I called. "Andrew!"

"Wait a minute," I said. "I have an idea." I ducked back into that crowd of people. I pushed past their legs. I ignored them when they cried, "Hey! Watch it!" When I was standing in front of the windows again, I looked from side to side. There was

Andrew. He was still staring at the winter wonderland.

"*An*drew!" I exclaimed. I hauled him back to Mommy and Seth.

Guess what. They scolded *both* of us.

"Do *not* let go of our hands," said Mommy. "Ever. Either of you."

"Well, not on the street," said Seth. "Or in stores."

"We have to stick together," Mommy went on.

And Seth said sternly, "Do you understand?"

"Yes," Andrew and I replied. Then I added, "Isn't anyone going to thank me for finding Andrew?"

Mommy finally smiled. "Thank you *very* much, Karen."

"You're welcome."

And Andrew said, "I *like* those windows. I am not tired anymore."

"Great," said Mommy. "How would you like to visit Santa?"

"Santa Claus?" squeaked Andrew.

"Right now?" I asked.

"Well, in a few minutes," said Seth. "We are going to another store. We will take a cab to it."

The taxi driver let us off in front of a store called Macy's.

"Macy's!" I cried. "I know about Macy's. They put on the Thanksgiving Day parade every year. Andrew, you and I always watch that on television. Santa Claus is at the end of the parade. And — and — Oh! I remember something else," I chattered as we entered the store. "I saw a movie on TV last weekend. I saw it with Kristy at the big house. It was called *Miracle on Thirty-fourth Street*. And there was this little girl who — "

"Karen," said Mommy quietly.

"What?"

"Settle down. You are wound up tighter than a tick."

"Sorry."

Mommy was right. I was not paying attention to anything. I was missing the sparkly gold and white decorations. I was missing the singers who were caroling in the store. But I did not miss Santa Claus.

Santa would have been hard to miss. About a million other people wanted to see him, too. They were waiting on a long line.

"Another store, another line," said Andrew. He yawned. But he kept craning his neck around to keep an eye on Santa. Finally he asked, "Is this the *real* Santa, Karen?"

I thought for a moment. Andrew and I had seen a lot of Santas that day. We had seen them on street corners. We had seen one in the train station. We had even seen a man in a Santa suit on the bus. I did not want to lie to my brother, so I replied, "I think he is another one of Santa's helpers. He is probably Santa's right-hand man. He must be the *chief* helper."

Andrew nodded. "Okay," he said. When it was his turn to talk to Santa, he said, "Hi, chief. Merry Christmas!"

9

Big Bucks

Andrew told the Santa Claus he wanted his very own radio for Christmas.

"Ho, ho!" cried Santa. "A radio! Okay, merry Christmas to you!"

" 'Bye, chief!" called Andrew as we walked toward the elevator. Then he turned to Mommy and Seth and me. He said, "He was pretty good for a Santa's helper."

"Hmm. You know what I just remembered?" I replied. "I just remembered that in that movie, *Miracle on Thirty-fourth Street*, the Macy's Santa Claus turned out to be the *real* one after all."

"Honest?" said Andrew, his eyes wide. "You mean I just met the real Santa? The real, real Santa Claus?"

"Maybe," I told him.

On our way out of Macy's we looked around the store. I had been keeping my eye out for presents for Hannie and Nancy. Most of the things we saw were for adults. I did see some kids' clothes, but the sweaters I liked cost over *fifty* dollars each.

By the time we left Macy's, Andrew was bouncing around like a pogo stick. He did not seem to need a nap at all. So Mommy said, "Let's keep going then. Let's not head back to the hotel yet."

Guess where we went. We went to that snowflake again. Well, not *right* to it, but nearby. Mommy and Seth wanted to look in this fancy hotel called the Plaza.

"Remember the story about Eloise?" said Mommy. "This is where she lived. In the Plaza Hotel." Mommy showed us a drawing of Eloise that was hanging in a hallway off the lobby.

After we looked at the fancy rugs and fancy lights and fancy hotel guests, we left the Plaza. We went across the street to a store called FAO Schwarz. It was a toy store.

"Perfect!" I said. "I will buy my holiday presents here."

But I did not. I did not buy anything. The toys were lots of fun. But most of them were way, way too expensive. I also did not buy anything in a place called Trump Tower.

"Everything costs big bucks," I announced loudly. I pouted.

"I think it is time to go back to the hotel," said Seth.

Meeting the Medvins

By the time we had returned to the hotel I felt better. That was because it was time to change our clothes and go to . . . Maxie's! Mommy and I put on dresses and party shoes. Seth and Andrew put on suits. But Andrew would not wear a necktie.

"Not even your clip-on?" asked Seth.

Andrew shook his head. Then he coughed. "They strangle me," he said. He coughed some more.

"Okay, okay," said Seth.

Maxie lives in an apartment building in

an area called the Upper West Side. When our taxi stopped in front of her building a man in a uniform greeted us. He opened our doors and asked us who we were visiting.

"We are here to see my pen pal, Maxie Medvin," I told him.

The man walked us into the building. Then we stood in the lobby while another man picked up a phone, pressed a button, and said, "Good evening, Mr. Medvin. Your company is here." He turned to Seth and said, "Name, please."

"Karen Brewer and family," replied Seth.

Finally the man let us go upstairs. "Apartment Fourteen-B," he said. "Take the elevator on your left."

My heavens. We did not even have to push a button when we stepped on that elevator. An elevator operator did it for us. I had never seen so many helpful people.

The elevator stopped at the fourteenth floor. We walked to apartment 14-B. Before I could ring the bell, the door flew open.

There stood Maxie. "Hi!" she shrieked. "Hi, pen pal! Hi, Karen!"

"Maxie!" I shrieked back. We threw our arms around each other. We shrieked until the grown-ups told us to settle down. Then we both tried to introduce our families at the same time.

Here are the people in Maxie's family: Maxie, her parents, Kathryn, Leslie, Benjie, and Doug. Kathryn and Leslie are Maxie's sisters. They are the twins. They are thirteen. Benjie and Doug are her adopted brothers. Benjie is two. Doug is only a few months old. They were born in South America.

Maxie showed me around her apartment. "Here is my room," she said. "I share it with Kathryn and Leslie. And here is the boys' room. That's my parents' room. There's the living room. This is the kitchen, of course. And this room is whatever we need it to be — the TV room or the playroom or the guest room."

We went back to Maxie's room. Do you

know what? It was not very different from my room at the little house in Stoneybrook, even though it was a bedroom smack in the middle of New York City. The big difference was the beds. In my room is one bed. In Maxie's room are two sets of bunk beds — enough beds for Maxie, Kathryn, Leslie, and a sleepover friend. But Maxie's walls are decorated with posters, like mine. The bookcase is crammed with books, like mine. The beds are covered with stuffed animals, like mine.

Maxie and I sat on her floor. We began a game of jacks. Then Mr. Medvin called, "Maxie! Karen! Time to go!"

"Time for Mamma Leones!" I said.

We rushed into the living room. Everyone was putting on their coats. Everyone except Benjie and Doug. They were staying at home with a baby-sitter. Then we stuffed ourselves into the elevator. Nine of us. I hoped that elevator was good and strong.

A Grand Lady

The elevator was just fine. It carried us safely to the lobby.

"On to Mamma Leones," said Mr. Medvin. He hailed two cabs. Mommy, Andrew, Mrs. Medvin, Kathryn, and Leslie squished into one cab. (Andrew had to sit on somebody's lap.) Seth, Mr. Medvin, Maxie, and I climbed into the other cab.

"Mamma Leones, please," said Mr. Medvin. "West Forty-fourth Street."

I had heard Mamma Leones advertised on the radio lots of times. The ads said to

enjoy a wonderful meal at a fine Italian restaurant and then take in the Christmas
show at Radio City Music Hall. (Or something like that.) I thought this sounded like
a fine way to celebrate the holidays. I was
very excited about our evening.

Guess what. The inside of Mamma
Leones reminded me a lot of New York
City. It was big and crowded and noisy. It
was perfect.

"Ooh," I said when we stepped into the
restaurant.

A waiter showed us to our table. It was
very long. (I think it was two tables pushed
together.) Four of us sat on one side, four
sat on the other side, and Mr. Medvin sat
at one end. Maxie and I sat next to each
other and pretended we were twins.

"Let's pretend we speak French, too," I
added.

"Okay," replied Maxie. "Voosee vahsee
chacha?"

"Oh, oui, non, vavoo, beebay," I said.

But then the waiter confused us, because he spoke Italian. Real Italian. He did not understand our made-up French. He barely understood our English. Real English. He wrote down our order, though. Maxie and Andrew and I ordered spaghetti. We just love fine Italian food.

I have never seen so much food in my life. It kept coming and coming and coming that night. Bread and salad and a plate of something called antipasto. (Andrew liked that because there were lots of olives, so he looked for one with a hole through it and tried to play it like a whistle.) Then we ate our main course, and then dessert. The grown-ups ordered coffee, too.

By the time we left, I was stuffed. And Seth said, "You could *roll* me to Radio City Music Hall."

At Radio City we found another crowd of people. Inside, we found even *more* people. People, people everywhere. When the ticket person had looked at our tickets, we

started to climb a flight of stairs. Up and up we went. I thought we would climb forever.

"How high are we going?" I asked Mommy.

"You'll see," she replied.

And suddenly we stopped climbing. We walked through a door. An usher checked our tickets and led us down an aisle. And I said, "Oh, my goodness."

I was looking over the edge of a balcony at the stage below us. Our balcony curved halfway around the theatre. Above us and below us were *more* balconies. All I could see were seats and people's heads and lots of red and gold. I felt like a very grand lady.

Then the show started. I was caught up in a Christmas world — Santa and elves and trees and presents. Plus, *real* animals paraded across the stage. My favorites were the camels.

"That was wonderful," I said to Maxie, when the show was over.

"The best," she agreed. "I am glad we could see it together."

"And I am glad we will see each other again tomorrow."

That night I fell asleep in my bed at the hotel. For just a moment, I remembered that I had not found presents for Nancy and Hannie yet. Then I thought, I am sure I will find them tomorrow.

Ice Skates

When I woke up the next morning, I looked around our hotel room. I still felt like a grand lady — even if I *was* sharing a bed with Andrew. (I do not like to do that. It is like sleeping with an eggbeater.) I wondered what we were going to do that morning. I found out as soon as Mommy woke up.

She said, "Karen, Andrew, do you remember the ice skaters we saw when we looked at the big Christmas tree yesterday?"

"Yes," we replied.

"Well, we could go skating this morning. We can rent ice skates there."

"Cool!" I exclaimed.

And Andrew raised his fist and cried, "Yes!"

I wanted to go skating right away, but Mommy and Seth said we had to eat breakfast first. We took the elevator to the hotel lobby, and we found a booth in the coffee shop. I love eating breakfast in restaurants. But that morning I was too excited to eat more than a few bites. So was Andrew. Mostly, he just played with the salt shaker.

Finally Seth said to Mommy, "We might as well leave."

Before I knew it, we were looking at the tree again. And soon we were lacing up our rented skates. All four of us. Mommy and Seth and Andrew and I. Seth helped me onto the ice, but then he let go of my hand. I am a *pretty* good skater, good enough to glide around by myself. I

watched the other skaters. I saw a man and a woman holding hands and skating together like skaters on TV. I saw a girl who could skate backward. I saw a boy practicing jumps. I saw a little kid in a fat snowsuit who kept falling — plop — on his bottom. Then I looked *up* and I saw a lot of people looking *down*. They were watching the skaters. I waved to them, and a few of them waved back.

Around and around I skated. I kept passing Seth and Mommy and Andrew. After awhile my legs felt tired. I slowed down. Then Andrew fell down. Mommy said, "I think that is enough skating."

We turned in our skates.

"Who wants to try hot chestnuts?" asked Seth. "A New York treat."

I had never eaten hot chestnuts, but if they were New York treats, then I would try them. "Me!" I cried.

Seth bought a little bag of chestnuts from a man who was selling them on his cart near the street. He helped me peel away the shell (it was *very* hot) and then I bit into the nut.

"Mmm, flavorful," I said.

We walked around and ate our chestnuts. I kept my eyes out for a store where I could buy my holiday presents.

"Hey! Look at that candy store!" I exclaimed.

Andrew and I gazed in the window. We saw an enormous chocolate Santa. It must have been two feet tall. A sign next to it said SOLID MILK CHOCOLATE. All *sorts* of wonderful chocolate things were in that window: a chocolate train and a chocolate Christmas tree and an entire chocolate village.

"Let's go in," I said. Maybe I would buy wonderful New York chocolate surprises for my friends.

Guess how much that Santa in the window cost. Sixty dollars. *Sixty*. Six-oh. More than one of the sweaters at Macy's. Well, for heaven's sake. I looked at some other things in the store. The smallest box of chocolate candies cost nearly twenty-five dollars. I decided Hannie and Nancy did not need chocolate. It would give them cavities, and besides, it was not very personal.

But what was I going to buy for them?

The Christmas Book

While Mommy walked around the candy store with Andrew and me, Seth stood outside. He was reading a newspaper. It had been delivered to our hotel room that morning. As soon as we left the store, Seth said, "I just read something very interesting. An author is signing copies of his new children's book today. He is signing them at a store that sells only children's books. And it is just a few blocks from here. Who wants to go? You could meet a real live author."

Of course we all wanted to go. (Even

though we have already met one real live author who visited a store in Stoneybrook once.)

The bookstore turned out to be wonderful. On the sign in front was a picture of Paddington Bear. Inside were books, books, books, everywhere we looked. Picture books and fairy tales and mysteries and books of poetry. Books about people and books about animals and books about science and books about sports.

Oh, boy. I knew we would spend lots of time in there. I did not know what to do first. I wanted to look around. I also wanted to stand on line to meet Mr. Arthur McBain.

Mommy solved the problem for me. "Let's get on line now," she said, "while it is still short." Then she picked up a book from a stack on a table. "This is the new story Mr. McBain just wrote," she told Andrew and me. "Why don't you take a look at it while we wait."

The line inched along toward a table at the back of the store. If I stood on tiptoe I could see the top of Mr. McBain's head. He had white hair.

"Maybe he knows Santa Claus," Andrew whispered to me.

"Maybe," I whispered back.

I read Mr. McBain's book to Andrew. It was about Christmas in a long-ago village, and talking animals, a shepherd, and a star.

When we reached the head of the line, Andrew said to Mr. McBain, "We like your book. Thank you for writing it."

And I said, "Will you sign it for us, please?"

So he did. Guess what. I can write cursive better than Mr. McBain. This is how he signed his name:

Still, a book signed by a real author is very special. I got an idea. "Mommy," I said, after we had said good-bye to Mr. McBain. "How much does the book cost?"

"Fourteen ninety-five," she replied.

"Darn!" I said. "I thought maybe I could buy books for Hannie and Nancy, and then Mr. McBain could sign them. They would be terrific presents. But I can only spend seven dollars on each gift."

"Well," said Mommy, "this book is a hardcover. Maybe the store carries some of his stories in paperback. They would not be so expensive."

But the store did not have any of Mr. McBain's books in paperback. They had lots of paperbacks — but none by Mr. Arthur McBain.

"Why don't you buy books for Nancy and Hannie anyway?" suggested Seth. "You could get some nice paperbacks. Books are great gifts, and you and your friends love to read."

"I know," I replied. "But I could buy plain old books anywhere. I want to bring Hannie and Nancy something *special* from New York. Like a *signed* book. Something I might not find in Stoneybrook."

"We have lots more time to look," Mommy reminded me.

"Right," agreed Seth. "Anyway, you are in New York to have fun."

I was trying to have fun. But I could not help feeling an intsy bit disappointed. I did not know shopping could be such hard work.

Magic Wands

When we left the bookstore, Mommy said, "Now Karen, we are standing on Madison Avenue. One of the best streets for shopping in all of New York City. Let's walk around for awhile."

"One of the best streets for shopping?" I repeated. I perked up. "Okay, let's hit the stores!"

"You can shop till you drop," Seth said.

And Andrew added, "You can shop until I say stop!"

We came to a store with a real carousel

in the window. But the store turned out to sell only lamps.

"Boring," said Andrew.

We came to a store with old-fashioned baby dolls in the window. But it turned out to be a furniture store.

"Pooh," said Andrew.

We came to a hardware store, a drug store, and a tiny grocery store.

"Monkey breath," said Andrew.

Then we came to a gift store. I knew it would be too expensive for me, but I wanted to look inside anyway. So we opened the door and walked in. A little bell tinkled behind us.

"Oh," said Andrew softly. "Look up."

I looked above my head. From every inch of the ceiling hung mobiles and wind chimes. The wind chimes clinked and clanked and bonged and dinged. I felt as if I could stand under them forever with my eyes closed, just listening. But I knew I had to find those presents. And I knew I would not find them in the gift store. So after

Mommy bought a Christmas present for Hannie's mother, we left.

I began to feel lucky because the very next store we came to — the one right next door — was a little toy store. It did not look too expensive. "Perfect!" I exclaimed. "I know I will find something here."

I looked and looked. I looked at every toy in that store. I found a terrific Troll, but Nancy already had one like it, and Hannie does not collect Trolls. I found some other things, too. But they did not seem *just* right. Finally I grabbed two magic wands.

"Are they what you *really* want to buy?" asked Seth.

"No," I admitted. I put the wands back. Then I burst into tears.

Toys

We left the toy store. Mommy hugged me. "Don't worry, Karen," she said. "You wil find something for your friends. I am very proud of you for not buying the wands. You are smart to wait until you find what you are really looking for."

"Whatever that is," I said.

"Chin up, Karen," added Seth. "It is time to go to Maxie's."

Maxie's! I had almost forgotten about our plans for the afternoon. My little-house family and I took a cab to the Medvins' apartment. Then Mommy and Seth left me there. They were going to take Andrew to the Children's Museum. " 'Bye!" we called to each other.

I turned to Maxie. "What are we going to do today?" I asked her.

"Maybe someone will take us to the park," she replied. "Mom?"

Mrs. Medvin was hurrying around the apartment. "I'm afraid not, honey," she said. "Your father and I just remembered something."

"What?" asked Maxie.

"The toy drive. It's today."

"Oh, my gosh!" cried Maxie.

"What is a toy drive?" I asked.

"Everyone in our apartment building," said Maxie, "has been collecting brand-new toys. Today we are going to give them to kids who do not have any homes."

"There is a center down the street," added Maxie's father. "Families who do not have homes can go there for help." Mr. Medvin was staggering around with a stack of games and dolls. The living room was beginning to look like a toy store.

"Santa Claus is going to hand out these presents," said Mrs. Medvin. "We have to take everything over there right away."

Mr. and Mrs. Medvin, Kathryn, Leslie, Maxie, and I each picked up a pile of toys. We called good-bye to the baby-sitter. Then we rode to the lobby in the elevator. We met a lot of Maxie's neighbors in the lobby. They were carrying toys, too.

The center was actually called the West Side Family Center. It was down the block from Maxie's, in an old, old building. Mr. Medvin led us inside to a room as big as the gym at my school. A party was going on there! Mothers and fathers and lots of kids were drinking punch and eating cookies and playing games.

"All of these people," said Maxie, "are homeless. They do not have enough money for a house or an apartment. So they sleep in shelters. Or sometimes they sleep here at the center. Or sometimes they sleep on

the subway or even on the street. The people at the center are trying to help them find homes. They help them with clothes and food and doctors and other things, too."

I could not believe that *so many* people did not have homes.

"Hey, look!" cried Maxie. "There's Santa. Boy, we got here just in time."

A man in a Santa Claus suit began handing out the toys — one to every kid at the party.

"Funny," said Maxie. "It is not even Christmas yet, and now these kids have gotten their presents."

"Won't they get more on Christmas Day?" I asked.

"Oh, no. I don't think so. Their families do not have enough money for presents. They do not even have enough for clothes. Or food."

"This is *it*?" I repeated. "These kids will only get *one* present for Christmas?"

"Some kids do not get any presents, you

know," said Maxie. "A lot of kids are not as lucky as we are."

I had thought being lucky was winning a big contest, or taking a trip to New York City for the weekend. I had not thought about being lucky meaning that I could sleep in my own bed in my own room in my own house every night.

I decided I was very, very, very, very, very lucky.

Guys and Dolls

Mommy and Seth and Andrew picked me up at the Medvins' late that afternoon. Maxie and I had to say good-bye to each other.

"I am glad I got to see your apartment," I told Maxie.

"Maybe someday I will see your house," she replied.

"I wish we could see each other again tomorrow. Maybe — "

"Karen," said Mommy. "Time to go."

Maxie and I hugged each other. Then we

waved and waved until the elevator came. " 'BYE!" we shouted.

My little-house family and I took a taxi back to our hotel. Mommy and Seth said we had to take a nap before dinner. All four of us.

"We have planned a big evening," said Seth as he stretched out on the bed.

I did not think I would fall asleep, but the next thing I knew, Mommy was shaking me gently. "Wake up, honey," she was saying. "Time to get dressed. Time for dinner and the show."

"Where are we eating dinner?" I asked sleepily.

"At a restaurant called Rumpelmayer's."

"Rumpelmayer's!" shrieked Andrew. "Just like the fairy tale!"

"Andrew. That is Rumpelstiltskin," I told him.

But when we sat down in Rumpelmayer's, I decided it was a little like a fairy tale. It was all pink and white. It was decorated with stuffed animals. Best of all, on the menu were plenty of things for children. And Mommy said we could order dessert.

"Rumpelmayer's is famous for its desserts," added Seth.

Here is what we ordered for dessert: a hot fudge sundae for Andrew, a butterscotch sundae for me, and something called cappuccino for Mommy and Seth. I thought cappuccino sounded very wonderful and special. Guess what it turned out to be. Coffee. I really felt that if Mommy and Seth were going to come all the way to Rumpelmayer's, they should order something better than coffee for dessert.

"Tell me again what we are going to do next," said Andrew as he ate his sundae. (He had smeared whipped cream all over his face.)

"We are going to see a show," replied Seth.

"A play with lots of music and singing and dancing," added Mommy. "It is called *Guys and Dolls*."

"In a theatre?" I asked.

"In a beautiful theatre," said Mommy.

We took a taxi to the theatre. (It was not too far from Rumpelmayer's.)

Seth handed our tickets to a man at the door, and we stepped inside. The theatre was not nearly as big as Radio City Music Hall. But I felt excited anyway. I looked at those rows and rows of seats, and at all the dressed-up people. My heart began to pound.

Later, when the curtain rose, I felt as if I were part of a story. I was out on the city streets, where *Guys and Dolls* takes place. And I wanted to sing and dance along with Miss Adelaide and Sky Masterson and Nathan Detroit and especially the man who was named Nicely-Nicely Johnson. The show was loud and wonderful. I hoped it would go on and on forever.

I do not know how Andrew managed to fall asleep during it.

When the show was over, Seth told the cab driver to take us to the hotel the long

way. He wanted to drive under the snowflake and by the Christmas tree in the dark.
So we did.

By the time I fell asleep that night, my
head was a whirl of music and dancing feet
and colored lights and ice cream.

St. Patrick's

"Time for church," said Mommy. That is how she woke up Andrew and me on Sunday morning.

"Church?" I repeated.

"Do we have to?" asked Andrew.

"Yes," said Mommy. "To both of your questions."

"But I guarantee," said Seth, "that you have never been to a church like the one you will see today."

Seth was right. He and Mommy took us to St. Patrick's. We had passed it several times in cabs. And we had walked by it on Friday. (I recognized it as soon as I saw it.) But we had not been inside it.

"Hmm," I said as we stood at the bottom of the steps to the doors.

"What?" asked Seth.

"I was just thinking," I said. "I do not know why people call New York an apple, but I know why they call it the *Big* Apple. Everything here is big. I have seen the biggest Christmas tree of my life. And Radio City Music Hall is the biggest theatre I have ever seen. The snowflake and the menorah are the biggest decorations I have ever seen. FAO Schwarz is the biggest toy store I have ever seen. And now St. Patrick's is the biggest church I have ever seen."

Seth grinned. "Actually, it is a cathedral. Come on. Wait until you see the *inside* of it." He began to climb the steps.

Mommy and Andrew and I followed. We tiptoed through a doorway. I stopped short. The windows in St. Patrick's were not plain old windows like the ones in our church in Stoneybrook. They were stained glass. I caught my breath. For a moment I could not take my eyes away from the windows. When I did, they fell on the rows of pews, the people walking along the stone floor, and the flowers by the altar. I knew I was in a place where I had to whisper, no matter what.

I tugged at Mommy's sleeve. "Can I have a quarter?" I asked her quietly.

"What for?" replied Mommy. "Didn't you bring your church money?"

"Yes, but I want to put a coin in the wishing well," I said, pointing.

"Karen!" exclaimed Mommy softly. "That is not a wishing well. That is the Holy Water. Now settle down and listen."

I realized that Mommy and Seth were not going to look for seats for us. We were going to stand up. We stood in the back of St. Patrick's. We watched and listened. After awhile, the only thing I could hear was Andrew. He was humming "Jingle Bells." And he was rattling the coins in his pocket.

Mommy and Seth heard him, too. "Okay. Time to go," said Mommy. "Put your church money in one of the boxes on your way out."

Andrew never has very much money. He is too little to earn money, the way I do. So mostly he just gets money on his birthday. On that Sunday, I knew he had exactly fifty-four cents. He put two dimes and a nickel in the box. I had $14.11. I put only one dime in the box. I did not think I could afford any more. I had not found presents for Hannie and Nancy, but when I did they would be expensive.

"Mommy, what time is it?" I asked as we walked outside.

"A little after eleven. Why?"

"When does our train leave? When do we have to go back to Stoneybrook?"

"In about two hours," replied Mommy.

We had not even packed our suitcases or checked out of the hotel. A funny feeling crept into my stomach. "We are not going to be able to go shopping today, are we?" I asked. (I already knew the answer to my question.)

Another Santa

Just as I thought, after we left St. Patrick's we returned to our hotel.

"Now do not leave anything behind," said Mommy as we packed our suitcases. "Check the drawers and the closet."

"Look under the beds and in the bathroom," added Seth.

"Boo, boo, boo," I grumbled as I crawled under the beds.

"Are you mad?" Andrew asked me.

"Yes, I am mad," I replied. "I promised Nancy and Hannie special New York presents and I did not find any."

"Maybe you will see something on the way to the train station," said Seth. "We will leave a little early so you can look."

"Thanks," I said. But I kept right on grumbling.

When we left the hotel, Seth asked the cab driver to drop us off two blocks from Grand Central Station. That way I could look in some stores. But a lot of the stores were closed. The ones that were open did not seem very interesting. Mostly they sold magazines and pocket knives.

"There are more stores in the station," said Mommy. "Remember, Karen?"

"Yeah," I replied glumly.

We struggled along with our suitcases. We passed a barbershop and a newspaper stand. I did not even glance at them.

"Well," said Seth a few minutes later, "here we are. Grand Central."

I sighed.

Mommy sighed.

And Andrew exclaimed, "Santa Claus!"

He was right. Standing by the door to the train station was a Santa. Actually, he was a Santa's helper. And not a very good one. He was skinny, and you could tell that his beard was fake. Also, I could see red hair sticking out from under his white wig.

Next to the Santa was a box with a hole in the top, like the money boxes at St. Patrick's, only bigger. A sign on the box said HELP NEW YORK'S NEEDIEST — PLEASE.

"What does 'neediest' mean?" I whispered to Seth.

"Poorest, I guess," he replied. "The people who need help the most."

"People who do not have homes?" I asked.

"Probably. And people who need food and clothes."

"And toys," I added. I thought about the kids I had met with Maxie the day before. I had been so busy since then — going to Rumpelmayer's and the theatre — that I had forgotten about the West Side Family Center. Now I remembered Maxie saying that the kids who were given toys at the party would not get any other toys for Christmas. And I remembered how lucky I had felt because I have a home. Because I have *two* homes.

Mommy and Seth and Andrew were hurrying through the door into the train station. "Wait!" I called to them. I set my suitcase on the sidewalk. I opened my purse. I pulled out my money — fourteen one-dollar bills and a penny.

First I dropped the penny in the box. Then I stuffed in a dollar bill. Then I stuffed in all the rest of the dollar bills.

"That's for kids who will not get any toys on Christmas Day," I said to the Santa. "Can you please use it to buy some toys?"

The Santa smiled. "I sure will. Thank you very much, young lady."

"You're welcome," I replied. "Merry Christmas!"

I ran to my little-house family. I did not know whether to feel happy or sad. I was glad I had given my money to the Santa. But I did not know what I was going to tell Nancy and Hannie about their presents.

Home Again

Mommy and Seth and Andrew and I walked through the train station. We found our train. Then we found four seats together. Mommy and Seth had bought coffee. They sipped it, and looked at a newspaper. Andrew fell asleep before the train even left the station.

I was tired, too, but I had thought of something I wanted to do. I asked Mommy for a pad of paper and a pencil. I propped the pad on my knees. Then I wrote:

DEAR MOMMY AND SETH,

THANK YOU FOR OUR TRIP TO NEW YORK! IT WAS GREAT! I HAD THE BEST TIME! THANK YOU FOR TAKING ANDREW AND ME TO SEE SANTA CLAWS, I MEAN CLAUS. THANK YOU FOR TAKING US TO ALL THE RISTO-RUNTES. THANK YOU FOR TAKING US TO RADIO CITY MUSIC HALL AND TO THE BOOKSTORE AND ICE SKATING. THANK YOU FOR TAKING US TO SEE GUYS AND DOLLS. THE NEXT TIME I BUY A DOLL I WILL NAME IT NICELY-NICELY JOHNSON EVEN IF IT IS A GIRL. THIS WAS THE BEST WEEKEND EVER. I WILL ALWAYS REMEMBER THE TREE.

LOTS AND LOTS AND LOTS OF LOVE, KAREN

When I finished my letter, I folded it in half. I slipped it into my purse. I would leave it in Mommy and Seth's room before I went to bed that night. Then I scrunched down in my seat. I fell asleep just like Andrew. When I woke up, the train was pulling into Stoneybrook.

"Home again, home again, jiggety jig," said Andrew.

We piled our things in the car and drove to the little house.

"We're here!" I cried as I ran through the front door. "Rocky! Midgie! Emily Junior! We are home!"

Midgie came skittering out of the kitchen. Rocky wandered in, yawning. (I guess we had disturbed a nap.) I hugged them and kissed them and patted them. "New York was great," I told them. Then I ran upstairs to my room. I knelt by Emily's cage. "Hi, Miss Rat," I said. "I am back. I can tell Nancy took good care of you."

I let Emily run around in my room for awhile. Then I put her back in her cage. I decided to call my two best friends. I called Nancy first.

"Hi!" I said. "I am back. Thank you for taking care of the pets."

"You're welcome," replied Nancy. "How was New York?"

"It was wonderful. The best, best weekend. We ate in restaurants. And we saw two shows. One was a play called *Guys and Dolls*. And this one man in the play? His name was Nicely-Nicely Johnson."

"Cool," said Nancy.

Then I called Hannie. "Hi!" I said. "I am back."

"Did you like New York?"

"It was terrific. We saw the biggest Christmas tree in the world. And the biggest snowflake and the biggest menorah. And we went ice skating, and I met Maxie's family."

"Excellent," said Hannie.

Later, just before supper, I unpacked my suitcase. Stuffed into one corner I found a small brown paper bag. Inside were the two I ♥ NYC buttons. I laid them on the bed. They looked very small. They did not look as if they had cost seven dollars each, which is how much money I had wanted to spend on my friends. Our holiday party was going to take place in less than a week. And I had no more money. I did not have New

York presents for my friends. I hardly had any presents at all.

I would have to figure something out. And I would have to do it quickly. I did not want to disappoint my friends.

Happy Holidays

I had a plan — sort of.

Nancy and Hannie and I had decided to hold our holiday party at the big house. My sister Kristy helped me decorate my room. We made a red-and-green paper chain and a blue-and-white paper chain. We hung them across the ceiling. We cut out snowflakes and taped them to the windows. We blew up some balloons, too.

Nannie helped me bake gingerbread men. They were going to be our refreshments — gingerbread men and hot chocolate.

At two o'clock on Saturday afternoon the bell rang. I dashed to the front door. I threw it open.

"Hello! Welcome to the holiday party!" I cried.

Nancy and Hannie had both arrived. They were standing on the stoop, bundled up in their snow clothes. They were each carrying two beautiful presents with big bows.

"Come on in," I said.

My friends stamped the snow off their boots. Then they stepped inside and hung up their jackets.

"What shall we do first?" asked Nancy.

"Open presents!" cried Hannie.

My friends raced up the stairs to my room. I followed more slowly. I watched them put their presents on the bed. Their presents were big. All four of them. The two I ♥ NYC buttons looked extra small next to them. You could hardly even see them.

In fact, Hannie did not see them. "Go ahead, Karen. Get your presents," she said. "Then we will open everything, one at a time."

"Well," I began. I paused. "Well . . . your presents are right here." I pointed to the buttons. Then I drew in a deep breath. "I have to tell you something about your presents. Remember, I had fourteen dollars when I went to New York?" I said.

"Fourteen dollars and sixty-five cents," spoke up Hannie.

"Right," I agreed. "I bought you these little presents in the train station when we first got to the city. Then I had fourteen dollars and eleven cents left. I looked and looked and looked, but I could not find just the right presents. Or else I found great presents, but they cost too much money. Then on Saturday, Maxie and I met these kids who do not have homes. They have no place to live. And I found out that lots

of kids like them do not get any presents at the holidays. None at all."

"Not *one*?" said Nancy.

"No, not one," I replied. "So on Sunday I gave all the rest of my money — the money for your presents — to someone who was collecting to help out New York's neediest. That is what his sign said. He told me he would spend my money on toys for kids. So . . . so those are your presents. I mean, your presents are that now some other kids will get presents."

"Really?" said Hannie. "That is so cool."

"Much better than another toy," added Nancy. "I got lots of toys for Hanukkah."

"And I will get lots of toys for Christmas," said Hannie. "Thank you, Karen!"

"Yeah, thanks," said Nancy. "That is the best present ever."

I grinned at my best friends. Then the Three Musketeers tore into the presents. We left a mess of wrapping paper on my bed. After awhile we put on our boots and coats. We built a snow family in the front yard. Later we ran inside. We ate our gingerbread men and drank our hot chocolate. We sat around the table in the warm kitchen and told jokes.

When the party was over, my friends and I called out, "Good-bye! Happy holidays! See you tomorrow!"

About the Author

ANN M. MARTIN lives in New York City and loves animals, especially cats. She has two cats of her own, Mouse and Rosie.

Other books by Ann M. Martin that you might enjoy are *Stage Fright*; *Me and Katie (the Pest)*; and the books in *The Baby-sitters Club* series.

Ann likes ice cream and *I Love Lucy*. And she has her own little sister, whose name is Jane.

Little Sister

Don't miss #45

KAREN'S TWIN

Audrey pulled me into the bathroom. She was still wearing the blue-framed glasses. She studied us in the mirror. "Hmm. Our hair does not look much alike," she said. (That is true. For one thing, Audrey's hair is brown.)

"You know what?" said Audrey. "I need bangs like yours, Karen. Would you give me bangs?"

"You want me to cut your hair?" I cried. "Oh, no. Sorry." I have gotten in enough trouble cutting my own hair. I was not going to cut someone else's. "I cannot do that, Audrey," I said.

I was not sure I liked being a twin after all.

LITTLE APPLE ®

BABY-SITTERS
Little Sister ™
by Ann M. Martin, author of *The Baby-sitters Club* ®

☐	MQ44300-3	#1	Karen's Witch	$2.75
☐	MQ44259-7	#2	Karen's Roller Skates	$2.75
☐	MQ44299-7	#3	Karen's Worst Day	$2.75
☐	MQ44264-3	#4	Karen's Kittycat Club	$2.75
☐	MQ44258-9	#5	Karen's School Picture	$2.75
☐	MQ44298-8	#6	Karen's Little Sister	$2.75
☐	MQ44257-0	#7	Karen's Birthday	$2.75
☐	MQ42670-2	#8	Karen's Haircut	$2.75
☐	MQ43652-X	#9	Karen's Sleepover	$2.75
☐	MQ43651-1	#10	Karen's Grandmothers	$2.75
☐	MQ43650-3	#11	Karen's Prize	$2.75
☐	MQ43649-X	#12	Karen's Ghost	$2.95
☐	MQ43648-1	#13	Karen's Surprise	$2.75
☐	MQ43646-5	#14	Karen's New Year	$2.75
☐	MQ43645-7	#15	Karen's in Love	$2.75
☐	MQ43644-9	#16	Karen's Goldfish	$2.75
☐	MQ43643-0	#17	Karen's Brothers	$2.75
☐	MQ43642-2	#18	Karen's Home-Run	$2.75
☐	MQ43641-4	#19	Karen's Good-Bye	$2.95
☐	MQ44823-4	#20	Karen's Carnival	$2.75
☐	MQ44824-2	#21	Karen's New Teacher	$2.95
☐	MQ44833-1	#22	Karen's Little Witch	$2.95
☐	MQ44832-3	#23	Karen's Doll	$2.95

More Titles...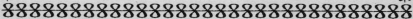

Available wherever you buy books, or use this order form.